COUSIN K

FRENCH VOICES

FRENCH
VOICES

COUSIN

K

YASMINA KHADRA

TRANSLATED BY
Donald Nicholson-Smith
and Alyson Waters

AFTERWORD BY
Robert Polito

UNIVERSITY OF NEBRASKA PRESS

LINCOLN AND LONDON

This work, published as part of a program
providing publication assistance, received
financial support from the French Ministry
of Foreign Affairs, the Cultural Services of
the French Embassy in the United States, and
FACE (French American Cultural Exchange).

French Voices logo designed by Serge Bloch.

Publication of this book was assisted by a grant
from the National Endowment for the Arts.

NATIONAL
ENDOWMENT
FOR THE ARTS

"A Great Nation Deserves Great Art"

Library of Congress
Cataloging-in-Publication Data
Khadra, Yasmina.
[Cousine K. English]
Cousin K / Yasmina Khadra; translated by
Donald Nicholson-Smith and Alyson Waters;
afterword by Robert Polito.
p. cm.
ISBN 978-0-8032-3493-2 (pbk.: alk. paper)
I. Nicholson-Smith, Donald. II. Waters,
Alyson, 1955– III. Title.
PQ3989.2.K386C6813 2013
 843'.914—dc23   2012035995

Set in Scala and ScalaSans by Laura Wellington.
Designed by Nathan Putens.

To my writer friends at the 813 Association
(Paris), the Étonnants Voyageurs festival
(Saint Malo/Dublin), and the Semana Negra
festival (Gijón). And to all my friends.

COUSIN K

For some people nothing turns out right.

Clumsy, they hold out a hand to their fellow man and put out his eye. They are sorry, but refuse to keep their hands in their pockets. They want to be useful; they strive to love everyone indiscriminately, not expecting anything in return, at times with an exaggerated sincerity that nothing can justify save perhaps their pathological need to feel capable of giving despite their destitute state. Their good will may be tarnished by their awkwardness, but their intentions seem quite unaffected. They stubbornly continue to turn the good feelings they harbor for others into evil: like morays, the kiss and the bite one and the same.

That is how Cousin K saw me: repellent even in my generosity. If I cannot forgive her, it is because she never understood a thing. And then, why forgive? Since the dawn of time forgiveness has never made wise men of those who forgive. One forgives only out of cowardice or cunning.

What did I blame her for exactly? For always looking on the dark side? But what did I offer, really, to change her mind? An uncalled-for gesture? A word better left unsaid? I failed in all my attempts to deserve her. My intentions were praiseworthy, but that was not enough. A good deed badly done is a doubly unpardonable wrong, first for its failure and then for the damage it brings in its wake. As for the evil deed that succeeds—what sweet success! All the goodness on earth cannot hold a candle to it.

Such was the battle that raged between Cousin K and me: good done badly; evil done well. We had no need to settle on who was wrong and who was right, or to point to where God's hand was and where the devil's; nor did we need to position ourselves in relation to our own truth (what is truth anyway?). The important thing was to follow our convictions wherever they led. Rightness is not a matter of what is correct but of what works: in this fight to the bitter end, it is not precision that prevails but effectiveness. When good is struck down by evil, that is proof that good has failed. And if winning does not cleanse the victor of his offenses, it does not spare the defeated either.

All the same, Cousin K was beautiful. When I think of her, her large eyes are obscured by her cruelty. Who was she? An angel? A devil? Both at once? What should I remember her for? Her grace or her villainy? The truth is, I can keep everything, just as I can reject it all. The choice is mine. Just as I am free to forget this story, I am free to tell it as I see fit. It is my story. I can give it any moral I like. Or none. Personally, I don't believe in morals. No contest can proceed without crushing them underfoot. That's my opinion; it's worth what it's worth, and I take full responsibility for it. Just as I take full responsibility for the story that follows. It's worth what it's worth as well; the rest—what others will think of it or do with it—is the least of my concerns.

Part I

In what
delirious
feverish night,
by what Goliaths was I conceived —
so big
and so useless?

Mayakovsky

I LEARNED TO hide when I was very young.

I wasn't afraid; no one was after me.

I was *hiding* whenever I was out of my mother's sight.

Every time she turned away, I felt that I vanished, ceased to exist.

I don't know what "through the looking glass" means. Yet if there are words that can convey the sensation I had whenever I found myself alone, it is certainly those. I had the sense of moving behind a two-way mirror: I could see without anyone suspecting I was there.

I didn't find this amusing.

I was even terribly upset by it.

I was not living; I haunted our house like a domestic poltergeist, provoking neither fear nor interest, perhaps on occasion merely an irritation that I never clearly identified.

And then, K came . . .

I had never seen anything bigger than her eyes.

I have never known anything harder than her heart.

The girl was, in and of herself, both night and day.

1

TIME PASSES AND waits for no one. All the moorings in the world cannot hold it back. Time has no home port; it is a gust of wind that blows on and never looks back. I mark off the moments mechanically. Like a clock. Noting the hour without lingering.

I am not really living. I am simply here, somewhere. A rut in the road, a name in the local register.

Nothing distracts me, not the clouds gathering above the mountain, nor the breeze dawdling amid the increasing stench, nor the kids learning the ways of the street, nor even the braying donkeys.

I consider noise an assault, I suffer the gaze of others like a violation, and every time I open my window onto the village I do violence to myself.

I don't like butterflies. Still, if they could move over and make room for me in their cocoons, I would offer myself up body and soul and sing their praises till Judgment Day.

My morning is as agonizing as it is futile: an island lost in a sea of renunciation. Its sun burns me; its prospect makes me nauseous. I get up, and then what? Go where, do what? My two-way mirror is my glass cage. I can pound on it until I pass out, no one will hear me. In any case, no one notices me. My morning is a desert where no soul stirs. It brings me nothing, I expect nothing from it; in this sense, we are even.

My night is a frigid and artless concubine. Her kisses raise welts, her fantasies are outlandish. As soon as the sun sets, she comes to me. In the same way, at the same place, at the same time. Without shame, without restraint. As vile as a reluctant orgasm. Dirtying my sheets and my flesh like a sow. Then, she withdraws. Ebbs away like the tide. Wrenching the blanket toward her. Abandoning me, naked and alone, in a demented déjà-vu world.

I'm not interested in hopping a moving train, in heading toward fresh disappointments. Nor am I awaiting the redemptive return of some Messiah. People unsettle me. Tomorrows do nothing for me. The turpitude of the world doesn't begin to affect me. I have no more respect for a dying dream than for the leaf of a plane tree turned brown by the fall. I stay behind my mirror, unassailable, curled up in my solitude, and listening—indiscreet, perhaps, but harmless . . . I listen to the night casting anchor in my insomniac soul, the wrinkles fissuring my brow, and the white threads of anguish weaving their web around my breath.

Imprisoned in weariness, in broken promises and dead years, I often peer at length into the half-light without knowing why, mounting watch over the silence for signs of I don't know what. I have no idea why I came into this world, why I *must* leave it. I asked for nothing. I have nothing to give. I am simply drifting toward something that will forever escape me.

My father died on the eve of the Great Day. I was five years old. I was the one who found him hanging from an S-hook in the stable, naked from head to toe, his eyes gouged out, his sex in his mouth. The cow had recently calved. Every morning at dawn I would fly from my bed to go see the little calf surmounting its unsteadiness. It was a magnificent animal, brown as a plowed field. That morning, it refused to come to me; it stood behind the bales of hay trembling, visibly terrified by the corpse hanging from the hook. I don't recall how long I stood rooted to the spot. Someone came to me, put his hands over my eyes and led me away from the nightmare.

I never went back to the stable to marvel at the calf's quivering. I had no more reason to go. I had become suspicious, mistrustful. Never again would I allow myself to become attached to what I could not protect.

Later, the villagers realized they had been wrong about my father. Flowers on his rehabilitated tombstone, posthumous tributes and acknowledgments, and all the sobbing of the keeners failed to convince me that "God alone is infallible."

I don't remember my father.

I have not suffered from his absence.

But I have not forgiven.

2

MY MOTHER was rich.

She was, in a way, the Lady of the Manor of Douar Yatim.

From deep within her fortress-like mansion, between the steles of her superb widowhood and the subjection of guilty consciences, she reigned over everything and everyone. People lowered their heads when speaking to her—they almost prostrated themselves. At first she was bothered by this; with time, she grew accustomed to all the bowing and scraping, the flattery of her courtiers and the taste of privilege; eventually she developed a malicious pleasure in looking down on her little world, the better to drag it through the mud. Her scorn quickly changed into cold animosity. I think she never really forgave the error that had led to her husband's execution. Twenty years on, his ghost was still there, ever more imposing. Sometimes, my mother would hold a hand out to *him*—and seemed to reach him. Her face would then light up with a fire fit to set the whole village ablaze. Meanwhile, she grew demanding, cantankerous; nothing escaped her gaze or the bolts it brought down on those caught in some transgression. One after another, the servants picked up and left. Even those who had been there for generations, who had once been in service with the retired Colonel Magivault and Madame de Bouvier.

Only the gardener had stayed. He had no family, no place to go. He was an old, sickly man, barely visible beneath his straw hat, moving about silently as if afraid of disturbing someone. He was solitary and unobtrusive; no one paid him any mind—which bothered him not in the least. He didn't ask for much. He liked to talk to the trees, sometimes to his dog, and tended the flowers with remarkable devotion.

He had died the year before. Noiselessly. Like a shade returning to dark oblivion.

After that, bramble bushes and wild grasses overran the garden paths.

My mother never knew what happened to the gardener. He died while she was traveling. When she returned, she acted as if nothing had changed. I believe she never even noticed.

My mother was unfathomable. She gave the impression of being able to face tragedy head on. Something in her died that morning in the stable where the young calf was learning to stand on its four legs. I don't know what exactly. And I don't want to know. I think it's her own business. I never caught her crying. Not once. Not for a moment. She was arrogant beneath her austere bun, her gestures dismissive, her gaze impossible to meet. I don't recall having seen her smile at *me*, either. Yet, strangely, whenever Cousin K curled up in her arms, my mother would suddenly find in herself the tenderness of the Virgin, and her inexpressive face would begin to radiate like a halo.

Never did her lips brush my cheek; never did her fingers smooth my hair. She didn't beat me, it's true; I lacked for nothing. We were together but did not know each other. I have no idea what that did to her; for my part, it was as if I had inadvertently landed in an empty circus ring: I was ashamed as many times over as there were vacant seats in the stands.

3

I JETTISONED MY childhood eagerly. It bored me. I hated school.
Its crusty old teachers and its unruly brats. A bench painted green
stood beneath a plane tree. The classrooms and the schoolyard
were on the other side of the tree, far away; I could almost believe
I was in the street. The pupils would be in an uproar, careering
about, chasing one another; from my bench, I didn't have to see
them. During recess, I would withdraw into my little exile; the
sound of the bell was slow to reach me there. Now and again
a ball would drop nearby. When someone came to fetch it, he
wouldn't even notice me.

Then came high school. In a neighboring city. They were hateful,
truly hateful, those high-school years. I have saved very few pictures
from that time: I see myself sitting in a deserted playground, or
standing somewhere with my hands behind my back and my head
in the clouds, or absentmindedly staring at my cat.

I don't have many pictures at all.

I have a married sister whose first name I sometimes forget,
a brother in the army, and that's all. No one comes to visit me,

I don't visit anyone. "Hell is other people," to be sure—but the damned can at least pick their ordeals. I retreat scrupulously into my tomb: I try not to interfere in the surrounding devilment, nor do I attempt to ward it off. I spend most of my time behind my curtains. Suffering the siege of the seasons. I watch as autumn lays my gardens low and winter strips them bare. I watch as spring mocks me with its magic tricks, as summer oppresses me with its scorching heat. And then it starts again: autumn, winter, spring . . . Oh, that I had ever been born! Life slips away stupidly, day after day, night after night, draining into a mere virtuality—drip! drip! drip!—that makes you want to fall asleep until death ensues.

Outside, the metal gate rattles in the wind fit to drive me mad.

Today—like yesterday, and no doubt like tomorrow—I carry on peering into the half-light without knowing why, standing guard over the silence and waiting for signs of I know not what. Rigid in my bed. Eyes closed, hands clasped on my chest, I am quiet and I wait . . . But time does not wait. Deaf as fate, blind as death, it revels in exposing the flimsiness of our futile struggles.

But to hell with time! When Cousin K is not here, hardly a thing is worth taking time over.

4

FROM MY WATCHTOWER, suspended between the lyricism of memory and the decay that goes with absence, I stare tirelessly at the chaotic village at the bottom of the hill. I try to trap the secrets behind the closed doors, to thwart the plots hatched amidst the twisting lanes; impossible, I can't do it. I imagine, one by one, the little people nibbling away at their slice of existence, harboring few illusions, bundling up their dashed hopes, consigning them to the junk room of disappointment; I feel no compassion.

The top of the distant mountain has been flayed; the river it secretes will never reach the sea. The countryside is arid, sullen, antagonistic—designed only to be withstood. The villagers don't like it. They curse it night and day. In Douar Yatim, every calamity that heaves in sight is merely the herald of an entire tribe. Neither sweat nor blood has managed to subdue this infertile soil. Come snow, come hail, the scree prevails across the years, while the exhausted eyes of the fellahs bespeak the gall of long resentment.

I count the hovels over and over, the scrawny trees, and the funeral processions. The other day someone died. There were not many people at the burial. Just a handful of men behind a rickety cart and two or three dogs in front, their muzzles scraping the path. A moment of silence and then no one to be seen.

When I was younger I would put on a black armband every Friday, line my eyes with kohl, and go to the cemetery. Someone is always buried on Friday. It is a day of prayers, opportune for giving up the ghost. Charlatans claim that on this day Satan mortifies himself. I had no eyes for either Satan or charlatans. Only the remains held my attention. No sooner was a tomb sealed than I began longing for the next one.

That was back when the gravediggers were charismatic, when the shovel disemboweling the earth filled me with a sense of surviving . . . a time when I would exult to see them die, those boorish peasants with yellowing teeth who tried to make me swallow the idea that a grave rehabilitated—more than a sin confessed—deserved forgiveness. Suddenly, though, I no longer needed to bury my Fridays along with those violet-blotched corpses. The ceremony spoiled the gravity of the moment: the same old chants, the same old hypocrisies. Over time, it didn't work anymore. The body is lowered and a curtain comes down: a man has died; it's not the end of the world.

In the lands of Islam, women do not attend funerals. Funerals are men's business. Exclusively. This used to infuriate Cousin K, and for my part, for a moment, I ceased hating myself for being a Muslim. Cousin K believed that the sky was within her reach, that the earth belonged to her, that she could do anything she wanted, and it didn't displease me to see her frustrated once in a while . . .

And yet, *the world has no one in it* whenever I happen to miss her. The woodland chorus itself is a dirge when her voice is not to be heard. The sun, the moon, the thunder, the universe, the entire universe is meaningless and mute when Cousin K is silent. Cousin

K is my reason for living. Her laughter is a symphony, the radiance of her eyes pure enchantment.

Whenever her gaze fell on me the phoenix would stir in its ashes. To brush her with my fingertips was to feel the pulse of eternity. Without her, I was nothing but a swelling bruise, a ripening calamity. Cousin K was my Northern Lights; I wintered well amid her petulance.

She left, as time leaves when a clock stops. Not a word to me, not a glance my way. Since then, no more Fridays, no more Sundays, only day and night; intolerable, inconceivable, yes—but the words are vain, inadequate. And then there is this thing that sticks to my skin like a shirt of Nessus.

5

FROM MY WINDOW I look down over the village, its back turned to the mountain. The shouts of the children reach me amid all the other sounds. Of all God's children, these are surely the most turbulent. They have even driven the patron saints of the place into exile.

A tractor gargles along the river. Its driver, tossed about on the seat, is gripping the steering wheel, his turban across his face. On the far bank, some peasants are returning to the orchards where they will spend the day waiting for evening to fall so they can go home. In Douar Yatim, ambition is a matter of longevity and nothing more.

On the road to the cemetery, a young man is playing with his dog. He flings a branch as far as he can, and the animal races to fetch it. The dog's tongue is hanging out, its tail jaunty; a slave to its master's age-old gesture. Now and again the two rush headlong into each other's embrace and exchange a flurry of affectionate blows . . .

I always hated my cat. He stole into my life, shamelessly setting up house, sure that at length I would accept the fait accompli. I was jealous when I saw how he garnered affection merely because he knew exactly how to stretch out near a hand and convert a simple reflex into an attentive caress.

There's nothing like a dog to make a man of you. If I'd had a dog of my own as a child, it might have had a different attitude toward me. But fate stuck me with this lame, deceitful animal that didn't even have the presence of mind to be there as my fingers merged into the growing darkness of night.

"THE ATTIC DOOR is getting on my nerves," says my mother, standing in the doorway to my room.

Her hair lies tangled on her shoulders. A bad sign. She tends her hair much as she tends Amine's career. With her hair undone, she is like a queen without a crown, though she seems not to care. The light behind her plays tricks with the contours of her body. She is fading, my mother. Inexorably. Dark circles sabotage the determination of her gaze. The corners of her mouth droop, eroding the former vigor of her orders and shouts. How brutal time's destructive work can be!

Then she vanishes. Without warning. As though swallowed up by the skylight at the end of the passage. Her gait, once so military, has lost its assurance; the rustling of her dress lends her a ghostly quality. I have the feeling she will evaporate if I hold my hand out to her.

I often wondered if I should I hold out my hand. Not once did I dare try.

6

I OILED THE hinges of the attic door, then went into my brother's room. Just like yesterday, and the days before. I opened the windows. I polished the furniture. Unthinkingly, I almost sat down in *his* armchair. My mother could not bear anyone to touch the belongings of her prodigal son. Even Cousin K would not venture up here. More than a sanctuary, my brother's room was a forbidden city.

My mother was miserable when her son neglected her. She did not know what to do with her hands or where to go next. Sometimes she would go into his room to gaze lovingly at his photographs, smooth his uniforms, inhale the scent of his pillow . . .

As for my brother and I, we got along fine. He would drape his arm over my shoulder all the time, and he loved me so much it puzzled me. But I used to think that *he too* would finally tire of me; I was wrong. He wasn't particularly observant, and rarely rebuked me. He was ready for anything, and he could always pique my curiosity. His eyes were the only ray of sunshine in the gloom of my childhood. They could not melt the ice altogether, but they brought a hint of warmth: not yet a spring—but a dream of spring.

I was happy when I was with him. I learned a lot of things. Had he stayed a little longer—through another summer, or a few short years—I would not be where I am today.

From one day to the next my brother abandoned me. He left for military school. I never got over it. I began to throw myself on my bed as one might throw oneself down a well, quite sure that no one would ever come looking for me.

My brother would come home on vacation strapped in his ash-grey uniform, beret tight against his temple, chin held high. Whenever he first got back, he wore a stricken look that said he was sorry to have left me in the lurch; when he went away, he could never shake off an embarrassed frown that said he was sorry to be dumping me yet again. He would wait for a gesture from me, for the slightest sign that I did not hold it against him. But my mother would grow impatient at the wheel, and he would twist around in the back seat, still hoping for the sign I never managed to produce. I watched the car draw away. Rigid on the front steps. Paralyzed from head to toe. Consumed with hate for my own arms that could do nothing at all except wrap themselves around me as though I might vanish into thin air.

I REMEMBER HOW, one evening in the manor when we were celebrating his first second-lieutenant's star, I climbed to the attic to destroy a portrait I had painted for him. I had planned to give it to him that day, but the guests had ruined everything: they laughed too loudly, they congratulated him continually—some even started calling him "General." My mother straightened his tie every time she kissed him.

Suddenly he turned round, and his gaze faltered before mine.

24

The joy instantly went out of his eyes. I could not get away fast enough from *his* celebration.

All evening long I crouched on the sill of the dormer window like a night bird. I watched the cars leave one by one. My head throbbed from the guests' laughter and banter and the slamming of car doors. Later, when the manor was quiet, my mother joined her son in the courtyard; they walked hand in hand until dawn. Welded together, their two hands were as one. Their bond embodied a faith that transcended every religion.

From my perch I watched them in their self-sufficiency, wringing my hands. Jealous, useless, I spat at the sky, not one of whose stars was of interest to me. Then I leaned a little farther over the window guard. I felt like throwing myself into the void. "Do it!" came Cousin K's voice. "Do it! I dare you!"

THAT NIGHT I resurrected my father in my mind's eye. Not that I missed him, but this was probably as good a way as any for me to commune with *his* solitude. I pictured myself at his graveside, waiting for his dust to stir. When nothing happened, I took sacrilege to the point of fancying myself God, frozen in the interstellar cold, sitting cross-legged high in a galaxy holding out my numb hands to the flames of hell and turning my back on this fetid piece of filth whirling in space like a worm screw and, infested by a humankind that bred like rabbits yet courted self-destruction, sullying my image by crucifying my prophets and boycotting my paradises. And as I surveyed the sweep of my splendid achievements, I fell wretchedly under the thrall of human sorrow and was suddenly fearful of the things I had created and that had escaped me, fearful of the oblivion that threatened my handiwork, fearful of the idea that, when the end came, I might find myself *alone*.

7

THE COUNTRYSIDE FINDS it hard to believe that the heat gripping it since morning will ease up once evening comes. But the humming of the white-hot earth slowly yields to the first stirrings of air among the vines. In the twilight's unsettling perspectives, despite the futility of a night oblivious to its dreams, the manor seems to withdraw into itself.

My mother has brought her rocking chair out onto the veranda. Her long hair streams down her back. She watches two sparrows frolicking around the fountain. On her knees lie her favorite letters, recognizable by the white ribbons she has tied around them. From time to time her milk-white hands clutch a few envelopes, and her iron-lady expression, in the setting sun, borrows a fold from her *litham*.

Previously she received regular news from *her* son. As soon as she spotted Amine's handwriting, her face would be suffused with a joy so intense that it cut me to the quick. She used to walk by me utterly absorbed in what she was reading. I could have screamed, upended the furniture, slammed the doors, broken the windows, and she would not have heard me. Once plunged into a letter signed by her precious Amine, my mother became unknown territory.

But for a while now the mailman has been afraid to meet her eye; the prodigal is no longer writing.

"What a beautiful sunset," I say.

She starts. Whenever my mother reacts like this, I feel ashamed. In my mind, the words I have chosen for her die like so many tiny sparks.

"Oh, it's you . . ."

She turns away, and for me it is like the waters closing over a tossed stone. The sparrows have worn themselves out and gone back to the orchards. In the distance, through the wide open gate, a group of women can be seen coming up from the river, washing piled on their heads and their littlest ones on their backs. The older children scamper ahead, noisy and startlingly energetic.

"Do you think," I ask, "he could be on maneuvers?"

She thrusts the letters beneath her shawl. Stealthily. She casts me an almost imperceptible menacing glance. I take refuge in the contemplation of my fingers.

"I miss him too," I pluck up the courage to add. "It's true we don't have much to say to each other, but when he doesn't come home like this . . ."

She brushes a strand of hair from her brow. Irritated now. "*He* is killing himself on the job."

"He likes what he does and he's very ambitious. He's an excellent officer. I'm sure he'll get a promotion soon."

"Don't tempt fate," she says superstitiously.

Once again she eyes me scornfully.

I position myself on the top of the front steps so as to have her neither behind nor facing me; so as to feel I am neither bothering nor ignoring her.

A miniature whirlwind swirls in the middle of the courtyard, performs a few last frenzied dance steps, and vanishes.

My hands are sweating, the tip of my nose itches; I feel ill.

Abruptly, my mother becomes angry.

"I'm *his* mama; I have my rights . . ."

I look at my feet.

I sense her distress but dare not share it; they say I am very awkward.

She pulls the letters out again, seeking comfort in them. Her hands tremble and her features harden. Suddenly she gets up and leaves. Before I can look up, she is gone. Only the rocking chair continues to sway, creaking softly. Never did an empty chair seem to me so full of reproach.

8

I HAD NEVER received a letter.

When I told Cousin K this, she claimed she wasn't in the least surprised.

I had just turned fourteen. That may not mean much, but there is no point in ignoring it.

It was a February day, brisk and unpredictable. It had rained in the morning, and the countryside was steaming under the afternoon sun. We were on the veranda. My mother was there. Cousin K was there. And there was that February day, but it didn't count.

"What would you like most of all?" my mother asked Cousin K.

And, sneaky as an attack of the flu, Cousin K replied: "It's not my birthday yet."

My mother took her by the shoulders and looked her straight in the face. "For me, you are born every day I see you. Now, I'm going into town and I don't intend to come back empty-handed. So, what would you like most of all?"

"Just you, Auntie darling," simpered K, glancing viciously in my direction.

Flattered, my mother clasped her close—so close that I hoped she would smother her to death. Riveted to the step, hangdog, I tried with all my might not to look toward them. Cousin K was waiting for that very thing to fasten her murderous gaze on me over my mother's shoulder.

When my mother left for town, K came over to me. The countryside recoiled slightly. The air held its breath.

"What about you?" she demanded. "What would *you* like most of all?"

I don't know why I answered, "A letter, perhaps . . ." She was thrilled. Usually, I didn't answer her. She took my hands in hers. For that gesture and that gesture alone I would have told my guiltiest secrets. When Cousin K takes you by the hand, she becomes your destiny.

"You see? I knew you couldn't be impervious to everything."

I was stricken.

She leaned toward me; her breath fluttered around my face. "A letter from who?"

I shrugged.

"From a girlfriend?"

I said nothing.

"I thought you trusted me."

"I haven't changed."

"So tell me. Who would you like to get a letter from?"

I felt as if I were getting smaller and smaller while she *invaded* me.

"See, you don't tell me all your secrets. Which proves you're always lying to me."

"I've never lied to you."

"Why should I put stock in anything you say? Before, you never hesitated. You were even happy to confide in me. You're not the way you used to be."

"You're wrong."

"All right then. So tell me: who from?"

"From anyone. Just a letter with a postmarked stamp and my name on it. The country it came from, the person who sent it, the number of weeks it took to reach me—none of that matters."

Cousin K rolled her sparkling eyes and asked me what I would like to find inside. I answered that maybe I wouldn't even open it. I would keep it sealed and be happy just to take it out of my drawer and stroke it now and again.

"You wouldn't even bother to find out what was in it?"

"No."

Intrigued and amused, she took a step back to see if I was serious; then she laughed in my face and vowed to send me a blank postcard just to rattle me.

9

THE SUN IS a spider's web with a cloud caught in it like a trapped gnat. Leaning my elbows on the windowsill, I wait in vain for any sign of a cooling breeze. Not a breath comes, not a whisper. The leaves in the trees are as motionless as thousands of idées fixes.

The muezzin's call rings out. My mother chooses this precise moment to come back from town. She drives her car into the garage by the fountain with its stucco guardian angel. The imam suggested she get rid of the statue because a hadith specifies that angels will not enter houses where there are dogs or images. To which my mother retorted that her niece K was *her* angel, and that was enough for her. The imam was furious, but he let it drop.

My mother is wearing a scout's neckerchief. This means that she has been honored yet again by the local militants. I had a scout's neckerchief once. My brother gave it to me. I never wore it, but it meant a lot just to have it. I hid it in a cubbyhole in my wardrobe, sure that no one would find it there. By some unknown magic, Cousin K eventually ferreted it out. She liked it and wanted to keep it. I hoped she would humor me a bit—allow me to think I was capable of *giving*. But when I pretended to want it back, she flung it in my face and pushed me against the wall, screaming: "I didn't ask you for the moon! Here, you can eat your flea-ridden rag for all I care! And don't you dare say another word to me ever again."

I was completely unnerved. This was not what I wanted; she had misunderstood. Watching her rage against me, I was panic-stricken. And as she wagged her finger, I thought that if God had chosen to make me anything at all except this puppet that a nine-year-old girl was tearing limb from limb, I would not have disappointed him.

MY MOTHER DASHES down the hall. She can never get back to her quarters quickly enough, and she is always ready to slam her door in my face. She slips her neckerchief off as she climbs the stairs. Her movements are jerky; she looks daggers at me.

I start up the stairs behind her. She stops halfway and turns to me. Her jaw is tight, her knuckles white. "Be a good boy. I forgot my purse in the glove compartment."

"Right away, Mama."

Her neck stiffens. She seems to panic when I call her Mama.

I go to fetch her purse and wait for her to come out of the bathroom so I can to give it to her. She finds me standing right in the middle of her room. Again her jaw tenses. She believes her room is a private domain and hates anyone entering unbidden. My brother, on the other hand, used to sprawl on her sofa. Keeping his shoes on. They talked loudly; he would leaf through a family photo album as she devoured him with her eyes. Sometimes, wrapped in her robe, she lay on the bed and let him massage her shoulders. He told her about military school, how strict the instructors were; she enumerated the plans she was dreaming up and all her great hopes for him. From time to time their confabs were punctuated with laughter, clear and genuine laughter—the laughter of two beings who were very close, needing nothing but each other to be happy: the epitome of mother and son.

And as the two became one, I would lurk in the corridor, watching them pay no attention to me for hours on end while I for my part never let them out of my sight.

"YES?"

"Your purse."

She motions for me to set it down anywhere. I hurry over and place it on her night table. Carefully.

"Do you need anything else, Mama?"

"Did anyone phone?"

"No."

Her head wobbles slightly. "You can go then."

I am dismissed. I nod and turn to leave.

"Amine?" she calls.

"Yes, Mama?"

Amine is my brother's name. She had made this mistake in the past. At first she used to apologize and call me by my own name. Then, little by little, as the slip recurred, she must have grown tired of correcting herself.

For a fraction of a second she looks at me in a way I find inscrutable. As a little boy, I suspected my mother of being a witch. She always knew everything that was going on in the manor. "Are you sure you're all right?" she asks.

"I think so. Why, did I do something, Mama?"

"I was just curious," she replies, already turning away.

UNTIL NIGHT CAME, in the depths of my room, bathed in a cold sweat, I couldn't stop wondering where I had fallen short, and why my mother wanted to know if I was sure I was all right . . .

10

ONE SWALLOW DOES not make a spring. One promise does not guarantee happiness. A visit from my brother did both. Whenever he came back to the house he exorcised its old demons.

By daybreak, before he was so much as a speck on the horizon, the universe would be seized by an uncommon feverish excitement. It was as though the gods had gone into a trance. The birds sang with all their might, the village dogs grew restless, and the air was weighed down by an indescribable tension seeming to presage some seismic event. Already my mother's footsteps could be heard everywhere. She went about slamming doors, summoning a horde of menials long since driven away by her abuse, and thundering up and down the corridors. Twice she came into my room to find me as mute and immobile as the furniture and raged against my indifference on *a day like today,* the only day that God made right—the day that her precious son had chosen for his homecoming.

Before long Amine was in the courtyard, splendid in his officer's uniform. So imposing was the figure he cut that sky and earth were alike obscured.

My mother could not contain herself. She had waited for this moment in pain. Her suffering was even greater now that he was here. Her eyes bespoke childbirth; her joined hands recalled the praying Virgin. She could move neither forward nor back. She tottered, she staggered, she reeled. She overdid it.

And then at last she broke free: "My hero!" she cried. And she flowed, my mother, she cascaded; she was nothing but lapping surf, foaming waves. Her hands—usually distant, restive—were now streams, her arms rivers; my mother was an ocean.

The two ran to one another, crashed into one another. Like two comets. It was a spectacular collision whose shockwaves made the walls, the hills, the very horizon pull back to clear a pure, unencumbered space for the two of them.

"My darling!"

"My mother!"

"My hero!"

"Mama!"

"My darling!"

"My mother!"

"My hero!"

"Mama!"

But Amine had not come alone. When at last the two celestial bodies drew apart, the world returned to its insignificance. My mother deigned to look over her son's shoulder and discovered a rival. In an instant the mirror broke, and so did the spell. Amine readjusted his tie, went to get his companion, who was waiting in the car, and pushed her ever so gently toward the iron lady:

"Mama, let me introduce you to Amal."

My mother remained calm. She did not extend her hand.

Amal registered the rejection coolly. She had the insolence of her youth; her eyes were hungry for battle.

"You could have warned me," said my mother.

"I wanted to surprise you."

"Indeed I am surprised. By your new stripes."

No sooner was my brother's back turned than my mother's face became a waxen mask. "You're wasting your time, my sweet," she whispered in the girl's ear.

Having opened hostilities, she regained her majestic composure and hurried to catch up with her revenant.

HE CAME INTO my room, took me in his arms. I don't know if he sat on my bed or remained standing; I can't remember. All I remember are his shining, limpid eyes, and how they grew troubled in my presence. But my mother called him right away, and robbed me of him.

IT WAS NOON, the hour when all activity halted in Douar Yatim. Silhouettes blurred, dogs fell silent, time stopped; in the twinkling of an eye, all life went out of the place.

My mother set the table up on the veranda. Three place settings. She put one chair next to hers, the other as far away as possible to make sure the girl was suitably exiled. Despite the good things my brother had to say about her, my mother refused to accept Amal. My mother felt duped.

She did not invite me to join them. It was impossible, she explained. That was that.

My mother dipped her spoon into her bowl and swirled her soup distractedly. After a moment of impenetrable reflection, she issued her pronouncement:

"You can't have your cake and eat it too."

My brother set his knife down on the edge of his plate and wiped his mouth with a napkin.

"Just what does that mean?"

"Attend to your career first."

"Ah."

"Quite so."

"And what exactly is a career according to you, Mama?"

"You sound like everyone else now. You're too young to think of weighing yourself down with a family. At your age, especially when you've already attracted the attention of your superiors, you should be working even harder to impress the higher-ups. Your colonel can't stop singing your praises. With just a bit more discipline, and if you stay away from all those little human weaknesses that in any case do more harm than good, I feel certain you'll rise higher than those fighter planes you fly."

"Mama, please. A barracks is not a monastery. There are generals with loads of children."

"You're not a general yet."

At this Amine threw in the towel.

The meal went on in stultifying silence.

My mother scrutinized the interloper's every gesture with the obvious intention of so disconcerting her that she would be put out of action. But the girl was not to be intimidated. Clearly this was by no means her first fight, and she had the self-confidence of someone who knew how to stick to the essentials, how to fight on her own ground with weapons of her own choosing. For his part, the young officer, amused and flattered to be the focus of so much passion, merely smiled. He forgave the one and made his excuses to the other. He was condescending, almost smug: in short, a spoiled child.

11

AMAL WAS BEAUTIFUL in the way women made for others know how to be. When she got up at first light the dawn itself could barely outdo her. Rather like Cousin K, she gave back to the manor what history had stolen from it.

Sitting beneath the locust tree, she resembled a sacred fruit fallen from a branch. Today she was reading from a collection of poems. Whenever her hand turned a page, you wanted to do the same. From time to time my brother whispered in her ear, and Amal would erupt in laughter so crystalline that no festive garland of mine could have sparkled more brightly.

My brother was born to be happy. All the good luck went his way. Including mine. But the way some things are meted out must not be challenged; the greatest proof of love is not to contest anything.

They were a magnificent couple; they seemed made for each other and they were fully aware of it. No squall, no cataclysm, one felt, could damage their idyll, much less destroy it. In the shade of the locust tree they hearkened to each other's dreams, she retailing her poems like petals in he-loves-me-he-loves-me-not, he keeping cadence with his eyebrows. It was as though the collection of poems had been written just for them: it resembled them in every way.

I say this not to denigrate their joy, but I have always thought that books are like funeral urns for the ashes of intimacies to which we feel entitled, secrets of which we turn out to be unworthy keepers. I read an enormous amount in my teens and twenties. Perhaps I was trying to master another sort of intrigue, that of writers, meaning those who, out of frustration with a prosaic reality, feel they can escape from it by borrowing something of the vanity and durability of myths. The more I read, the more clearly I became aware that writing amounted to a self-defeating enterprise, an attempt to ride the whirlwind, and above all that it was the pathetic expression of a split personality: perfect training for the most poisonous arrogation. I read as if I were unburying hateful truths, the phantom traces of my own torment, so that in the end I no longer knew who was haunting whom, who was dust and who vapor, who flesh and who spirit. And, just like a writer, I wanted to become my own character, a pompous way no doubt but a less foolhardy one of becoming one's own god. I had taken a schoolchild's exercise book and begun to cover its pages with interminable prose. I never reread anything. Once purged, my inner world, like vomit, left nothing behind but a foul aftertaste. Just like Cousin K's lies. After closing up my book of writings, I stuffed it away amid the old junk in the attic and never went back to it.

To this day I cannot fathom why my brother and his girlfriend did not do likewise. What good did they see in those poems and their startling naivety, always searching the stars for what lay within such easy reach?

AMAL WAS IN the back bedroom just across from my mother's. My mother had insisted on this. She wanted to keep an eye on her, and protect her precious little boy. If she left her door ajar, she would be alerted by the slightest rustle. Nevertheless, I went to see Amal sleeping every night. I would sit down in the chair next to her bed, jealous of the moon and the bands of light it cast across her body like so many unpunished caresses. When Cousin K fell asleep, there had been no one left in the world but the two of us. So deep was her sleep that I did not hesitate to kiss her on the mouth. Amal's sleep was a marvel. Over and over again the urge to take her hand set my heart trembling, but I did not give in. Ever since K had gone, I could never find excuses for giving in to temptation.

A RESTLESS SWALLOW, my brother left at dawn, taking his springtime with him. I can still hear the voices, the laughter, visualize the bright swaths of daylight, the figures like wisps of mist—a whole fairy tale detaching itself from the walls of the manor and abandoning the place as though inhaled by the fast-disappearing car. The grandest of dreams lasts no longer than a sigh; the slightest thing transforms it into a pipe dream. As the rumble of the engine faded, the landscape itself became barren. I looked over at my mother, waving her handkerchief on the front steps. Her suffering revived my hatred. *Turn around*, I begged her from my innermost depths. *Please, turn around. This is not the end of the world, Mama. He is not the only one. For the love of heaven, just turn around and look over here . . .*

She did not turn around.

In the distance the sun was basking in its divinity; I dared it to bring light to my mother's eyes. But there are shadows that can survive the flames of hell, and the shadows of the human soul are the deepest abyss of all—so deep that the very fingers of the Lord could not reach them. Not to be outdone, the wind began to play its own tricks, ruffling the trees, rattling the vine trellises, raising clouds of dust along the roads, stirring up a host of teacup tempests.

My mother slumped onto one of the front steps and took her head in her hands. People always take their head in their hands when they lose control. But what did my mother really know about suffering? A son's departure? No letter in the mail? And because I perceived her pain so clearly, I refused to feel compassion.

I took refuge behind the curtains at my window. I liked seeing my mother suffer. It was one of the rare moments when I felt she was made of flesh and blood. But for how long? Soon she would be back on her feet, battle-ready and determined to overcome this moment of weakness and stop making a spectacle of herself. Suddenly, seeming to guess what was going through my mind, she turned and gazed up at my window. Whether she saw me I could not tell, but the look she cast in my direction caused the hairs on the back of my neck to stand on end. I shrank against the wall and made myself as small as I could.

"Hee! Hee! Hee!" chuckles Cousin K from the other side of the mirror.

Part 2

How divinely vault and arch
here oppose one another in the
struggle: how they strive against
one another with light and shadow,
these divinely-striving things.

NIETZSCHE, *Thus Spoke Zarathustra*

12

FRIDAY AGAIN, WITH its migraines and its suppressed yawns. A day tragic in its nothingness, hollow as a fast, sterile as a sleepless night. There is no funeral procession today to help one penetrate the torpor, which only adds to the misery of the stay-at-home.

I considered paying a visit to a certain old abandoned farm and braving the sight of a well where my mind was still held hostage to a child's act. Then I heard Cousin K: "I dare you!"

I did not dare.

My room gnaws at me like a guilty conscience; its stout-legged chests of drawers, its bronze heraldic shields and its overstuffed chairs fuel my discontent.

Beyond the French windows lie the misshapen hillside; the blighted fields; the tattered trees where the night winds whistle their unbearable litanies; the clusters of old men shriveling in the sun, chin in hand and eyes heavy with perpetual drowsiness; and there, at the end of all roads, all expectations, the cemetery.

I hate this place.

I can never be too wary of this village where nothing is left, where, instead of growing up, the dwarfs who dwell here merely grow old. The young have gone off to chase unicorns. Those who remain shun their meager flocks and the thanklessness of their land; their souls have gone to ruin, their faith is a disaster, and they have nothing left to love.

I look everywhere for a face, a glance worthy of interest: nothing. When nobody is being buried on a Friday in Douar Yatim, everyone goes to ground. Once prayer is over, no one lingers in the street. The town instantly has the feel of a ghostly territory animated only by the malevolent chirring of the cicadas.

It is summer. The long summer of the Maghreb. A relentless furnace melting all initiative and a leaden sky that no magic or incantation can dispel. Not a leaf stirs, not a bird sings. The sparse olive trees, confining orchards and minds alike, resemble torture victims; they mark out devastation all the way to the gates of hell, boxing off the poverty of those who can take no more. I have always been afraid of olive trees: they are twisted trees, witch's trees; their shade is a trap you can never escape. And then, beyond madness, as far as the eye can see in every direction, is silence, struggling to replace time . . .

My mother is gone, who knows where. She doesn't need to tell me where she goes. Yesterday was her birthday. I put a flower on the mantelpiece, just where she keeps her keys. This morning, I found the flower in the same place, drooped and dying.

Cousin K was lucky. When she "forgot" something, she was treated all the more tenderly. *It's not so bad*, is what they whispered to her. *It's almost as though you had remembered; after all, you are our most precious gift.* The pendant I had slipped under my mother's pillow was mine—and Cousin K knew it. Yet she said not a word when my mother thanked her for it. She simply crossed her fingers and blushed—not from shame, but as befits the fiend she was. Cousin K had the scruples of a snake. But who would dare suspect it?

God, how I miss her! Her absence is the one and only thing that cripples me. Without her, I am nothing but a swelling bruise, a ripening calamity.

Opening the windows wide cannot lift my spirits. The books lying about no longer mean much of anything to me. I stride up and down the corridor, going into one room after another; I desecrate the bedrooms, violate their secrets, opening armoires as though they were trapdoors. *Nothing!* The world is a silence broken by the barking of a stray dog. I know the bark of every dog in the village.

To leave the manor is to feel the oppressiveness of Douar Yatim. Not a living soul abroad. Grotesque doors, bricked-up attic windows, a motionless donkey by an overturned cart, and the local cafés on every corner quite dead, shuttered and padlocked, and painted an orange as startling as sin.

I cross the village. Silently. Never stopping. Never even turning to look back. Walking, walking—to the river. On the opposite bank an age-old olive tree taunts me. It looks like a stricken hydra. Once, long ago, it was *my* tree—my tree in the days when I had a cat. As a child I set up a swing beneath that tree as a way of enticing Cousin K. But the sight of it did not make her jump for joy. She was even indignant.

"You mean you dragged me all that way for this?"

"The ropes are solid. I've tested them."

Cousin K couldn't care less about the ropes. She found my handiwork pathetic. As she went off, irritated, she shouted back to me that I had the imagination of a cow. I was stunned. I did not understand, but I was as terrified as I was dumbfounded. Prostrate at the foot of my tree, my chin on my chest, I had to wait until nightfall to go home for fear of how she would look at me.

Later, laughing wolfishly, snot-nosed urchins arrived and tore my swing to pieces. I watched them at work from my window like a gargoyle gazing out over a sinkhole.

That was when I began to be afraid of olive trees.

I SETTLE DOWN beneath the tree and close my eyes.

An hour goes by, maybe two. In the desert of my solitude, time exists but does not matter. A breeze sets the brush astir. Far away, the sun is about to give up the ghost; pitching downward in slow motion, it impales itself on the mountain peak without a murmur or a jolt, scattering dabs of glitter over its surroundings. Soon now, the heat of the day will be spent; people will have to emerge from their burrows, minds rife with muddled dreams. Soon, swarms of children will infest the square, shrieking and destroying, as great a threat to the trees as the goats, as inimical to the old men as bouts of heartburn. Soon, the café will come alive with the clinking of dominoes, and, in my mind, its uproar will add to the mad rattling of the gate in the dark. Soon, I will be frightened by the unnaturally long shadows; and I'll be afraid of my hands, of tremors that fray my nerves and of the feeling that paralyzes me when I lose control of things . . .

And then I see her! Thrust from a car, hair in disarray, veil twisted about her legs, she is begging, screaming, clinging to the car door. The driver keeps pushing her away. She tries to grab his arm, runs and runs and then stops, staggering, defeated, overwhelmed. The car disappears behind a low wall. The girl plunges her head into her hands and collapses. Oddly, the village turns its back on *us*.

13

"It's not a good idea to hang around here," I say to her.

She starts, and pulls her skirt down when she sees me pop up like a genie in front of her. Cousin K used to hate my popping up like this. *Like a genie.* She would try to shake me off, but in vain: in the end I always managed to track her down. I knew her haunts, her hidey-holes, and her little weaknesses perfectly, but my intention was not to expose her or be disagreeable. I was not spying on her, not following her; it was enough for me to think of her, and she would be there. As simple as that. As though I had made her with my own hands.

The girl stares at me. Her skirt, still askew, disturbs me. I try to look away but fail. She looks around fearfully; her hands are not still. My pallor bothers her; it is my natural coloring, but the doctors have never been able to account for it.

"Don't be afraid."

My childlike face seems to reassure her now. My primary-school teacher used to confess that he found me pretty—pretty as porcelain—and his voice quavered oddly as he said so.

I point the manor out to her. It stands slightly apart from the village—as though the colonist of old wanted to keep his distance.

"That's where I live."

Putting her veil back in place, she rises and makes as if to leave. I hold her back, grasping her by the hand without recognizing my own, startled by my gesture. My voice reaches me from very far away, breathless:

"Please . . ."

"It's getting late. I have to go home. Think you could help me?"

Her words electrify me. Never before has anyone asked me for help. Except for Cousin K begging me to help her climb up on the armoire. It was her idea: *she wanted to sit on a throne, play the sultaness.* I had no desire to go along with her. Too dangerous. But she insisted. Her foot scratched my cheek; she did not notice. Her throne was the only thing she had in view. She loved to see the world at her feet. When she was caught on top of the armoire, she blamed me without a second thought: *It was him. I didn't want to. He made me do it.*

Why was Cousin K always lying?

"Doesn't a bus come this way?"

"I don't think so."

"Or someone who could take me home? I could pay them."

"I hate driving, cars make me nervous. You shouldn't hang around here though. The villagers loathe strangers."

My expressionless voice nags at her from behind.

"I saw a taxi a while ago," she insists.

"Never after sunset. Around here no one travels at night. It's bad luck. You'll have to wait till tomorrow morning. If you like, you can come to the manor."

She hesitates.

"If you don't trust me, go back on the road. A truck might come along."

I walk away. Disappointed. When Cousin K hesitated, it meant a refusal; it was she who taught me not to push it.

I have gone about a hundred paces when she comes up behind me, out of breath.

"Hey, don't leave me."

"I was leaving you be, that's all."

Her fingernails dig into my wrist, hurting me.

"I trust you," she says.

In the far distance, halfway down the road to no return, an ass's sudden bray is quickly echoed by the yapping of roving dogs.

The sun has gone; the village is veiled in shadow, then plunges into complete darkness. Only the manor still stands out against the sky like an enemy fortress.

Another Friday flying away swift as a bat. The hobgoblins are already massing in dark corners; the early sounds of night promise a stormy watch.

14

I SHOW HER into *his* room and then withdraw, careful to close
the door behind me. I have been fascinated by such exits ever
since the time my mother had all those servants at her beck and
call. Back then, a valet would come and bustle about my bed, deft
and efficient. Then he would withdraw, walking backwards with
eyes cast down; there was an arrogance about his servile attitude
that I could neither identify nor justify. He spoke hardly at all, was
ever on the watch for any sign of an order, and when my mother
addressed him he sprang to attention with an obsequiousness
so provocative that I despised him.

That evening as I leave the unknown girl's bedroom, and later
as I return bearing a cold meal on a tray, I have a vague sense of
infringing the proprieties and hence of eliciting contempt.

I place the tray on the bedside table.

The girl thanks me.

"If you would like to cook something, feel free. I'm clumsy with
fire."

"No, this is just fine."

She is sitting on the edge of the bed, feet on the floor and hands clasped in her lap. From time to time she looks up, at once fascinated and intimidated, to contemplate the luxury that assails her. It is apparent that she is unused to high ceilings. The room's immensity, the gigantic lamps dangling above her, and the fresco with its faint play of light all conspire to disconcert her.

"This is Amine's room," I inform her.

She seems unable to gauge the scale of the sacrilege involved, indeed does not even suspect it; nor does the tremor in my voice alert her. Since I left she has not budged an inch for fear of disturbing the order of things by the slightest quiver. Her gaze slides hurriedly over the furniture as though the setting evokes an extreme reserve in her. For my part I shudder at the depth of the desecration, but *for the first time ever* I do not back down.

The girl keeps smiling. People often smile when they don't understand. Her timidity, like her worn-out clothes, shows how deeply countrified she is, an impression reinforced by the almost clownish effect of ill-applied makeup. Her ring has long since lost its cheap allure and her earrings are startlingly artless. She is just a wretched peasant with bitten-down nails, a child of poverty who might have been ordinary were it not for the traces, deep in her eyes, of degrading compromises.

"Please relax, Mademoiselle."

"I'm quite relaxed, thank you."

"That's good."

I leave the room.

When I return to clear away, I find her in the same spot, in the same position, still staring at her glorious surroundings. She has not touched the tray.

"You haven't eaten anything."

"I'm not hungry."

58

"Perhaps you'd like something else?"

"No, no, really, please don't go to any trouble. I'm not hungry."

And she smiles.

Again!

There is nothing more misleading than a woman's smile: it is a poisoned fruit, a subtle confidence trick. Cousin K's smile used to alarm me: it meant the trap was fully set. As cautious as I might be, as eager to keep my mind focused, I had no prospect of escape.

I pick up the tray.

"It will be a long night. Should you need anything at all, tap twice on the wall. I am just next door."

"Thank you. You're very sweet."

How repellent her familiarity is!

If only she would deign to touch the meal I have prepared for her with a devotion that would have thoroughly perplexed my mother!

I hurry out, returning to my room and the cravings of my bed, the desolation of my ceiling . . . and to *waiting*—that other tapeworm threading its laborious, sinuous way into the seething anger that I should have been spared.

15

WAITING IS MY island of predilection. An island whose horizons have been thrust away, stripped of their charm, relieved of their function. This is my own private penal colony, where I am both convict and jailor, with no prospect of pardon or parole: a penitentiary with no gallows, no visiting room, just a sentence to serve with the calm obstinacy of a guilty man who is his own judge . . .

Midnight . . .

One in the morning . . .

Two . . .

Outside, the full moon struggles to reinvent daylight, while the chirring reaches an inconceivable pitch.

Stretched out on the bed, I gaze at the ceiling lamp.

I hate ceiling lamps; their milky glow is so artificial. I prefer candelabra with their martial aspect; their dim light is so adept at luring moths, those pale imitators of Icarus. I have a candelabrum in my room, most imposing with its brass trappings. Its flickering aura can disguise the shadows and flush out the gremlins that lurk in dark corners. Sometimes, when sleep will not come, I need only concentrate on the will-o'-the-wisps fluttering around its branches, and I drop off right away.

Tonight, though, I make a point of not looking at the candelabrum.

Tonight I have no wish to sleep.

I wait . . .

As far back as I can remember, no creature has ever seemed as close as the girl ignoring me in the next room. The fact is I have no girlfriends; very likely I never shall. I have always avoided girls, detecting in them a kind of bitter frailty, a latent martyrdom.

There was a time when I had a cat—the time when olive trees inspired me. He was a calculating cat, prone to positioning himself within reach of my hand and passing this opportunism off as affection for me. He was no friend to me; we lived together, that's all. I did not drink, or smoke; the cat was there, and gave me something to do. Until the day, that is, when he scratched me. An absurd act, impulsive, reckless . . . That cat was never seen again.

At fourteen I wanted to fall in love with a girl cousin. Her parents used to come to the manor over the holidays to escape the clamor of the city. They were well-to-do people. They liked to picnic by the riverbank and stroll through the orchards, and came back to the house only after nightfall. They had a little girl, and it was Cousin K. Beautiful. Enormous eyes. Silver-blonde hair. She was a tune played on the flute, a sliver of joy, and she glistened like a lake of dew. When she went to bed, the night itself so missed her that it put on mourning clothes till dawn.

Cousin K and I liked to haunt a derelict old farmstead on the other side of the hill. There were tumbledown cottages there, open to the four winds, and a well. Hardly paradise, perhaps—but Cousin K could have turned a cowshed into a caravanserai or a spider's web into a hanging garden. To see her playing was a dream. I would tag along behind and watch her. I did not play; I was too awkward. I was content to follow her, smile when she smiled, and scurry after her when she ran. When she tired, she would sit on the coping of the well and spend long moments staring down into the pit. She cried "Yoo-hoo!" and burst out laughing when the echo came back. "It's fantastic! Look, isn't that the other side of the world down there?" But when I came up to the well to look down, she would push me away. Sometimes she would drop pebbles and listen for the cavernous plopping sound they made on hitting the water.

One day, as she was yelling stupidly down the well, I came up behind her and pushed her in.

I went back to the manor as though nothing had happened. Not that I was unaware of my act; simply, I felt I had no reason to regret it.

They found her at the bottom of the shaft, her leg broken and her eyes bulging with terror. She went mad, and has still not recovered.

They say she spends her time going back and forth between clinic and asylum and is terrified of the dark.

I have never seen her again either.

Whenever I think of her I feel sorrow, but what distresses me most of all is that to this day no one has ever suspected me.

16

THE CLOCK STRIKES three. Distinctly. I begin to pace up and down, arms crossed over my chest. What was holding up the dawn? My sleepless night? What was making me doubt a promise still not kept? What was grinding down my patience like asparagus root? *Waiting!* A treacherous companion. Waiting is what strips the shadows, dispossesses the silence, terrifies those who are alone and shapes their madness . . .

Why doesn't she knock?

She has to knock.

She is not knocking.

I go out into the corridor and walk up and down from one end to the other. In my head, the well from my childhood is moaning. And I think of that cousin, so full of herself, so venerated by everyone. No sooner did she arrive at the mansion than the whole earth rejected me. All eyes were for her. *She is brilliant at school . . . She walked off with all the prizes . . . A prodigy! Dear God, what kind of angel have you given us in this girl? . . . An angel—and one reborn with every day God sends! . . .* What about me? I was rotting on death row; I could disappear or throw myself down in front of them, but if I grabbed the moon and presented it to them on a platter, they would tell me to be careful of the platter and fail to notice the moon. As they gravitated around her, I realized, even at my unphilosophical age, that the blind man is not someone who cannot see but someone who is not seen: there is no greater blindness than to go everywhere unnoticed.

Cousin K said I looked like a hanged man with my hunched neck. She made fun of me, tormented me. With her skirt hitched up above her pink knees, she would pick slowly, interminably, at a dish of delicacies, taking tiny, corrosive bites; she loved to humiliate me, to see me hold out my hand. *Yum! Dee-lish-ious! These raisins are so soft that you don't even have to bite into them. Auntie is ever so kind to me. She has promised to make date syrup just for me; you'll be green with envy.*

I would sooner have desecrated a tomb than think of raising a hand to her. She was the family's sacred jewel, their very own little god. One had only to see them brushing her hair. Cousin K let them do it, her white hands in her lap, greedy for attention, fully aware of the pleasure she was affording.

They called her an angel.

She was no angel.

K was mean and self-centered, rancorous, spiteful. A she-devil. Having no fear of disappointing, she did as she pleased. The missing jar of honey was her doing. The profanities in the cowshed were hers too. But inevitably, automatically, they put the blame on me.

I hate them.

I hate her.

17

I PUSH THE door open. Angrily.

She awakes with a start.

"Why?"

She still refuses to understand.

"Why didn't you knock?"

"I don't need anything."

I took my head in my hands.

"What? Who do you think you are, saying that you want for nothing?"

"I . . ."

"Be quiet! Nobody has everything they need. There is always a need somewhere, something overlooked, a nagging lack of some kind or other. It's no use telling yourself that everything is fine, could not be better, because it's just not true. It doesn't matter whether you live in a palace or a hovel, dress in silk or in rags, whether you are revered or reviled, you are bound to need something, or someone. You long for a glance, a word, a sign, and often your most fervent prayers go unanswered. Why? Because that's how it is. There's no point in looking for the flaw in oneself:

the flaw is in everyone, in all the questions we ask ourselves that get us nowhere . . ."

My index finger projects my anger:

"*You* are nothing at all. Until tonight you did not exist. It was I who made *you* up!"

My hands sketch the act of conceiving her, inventing her.

"You are going to knock. It is imperative that you summon me."

I am insulted, diminished. My head crackles; spasmodic flames lash at me, engulf my very soul, reach to the core of my pain; I am a human torch, a pillar of self-torment.

She kneels on the bed, wild-eyed, as though encountering me in a bad dream.

"Don't look at me like that, for the love of God, don't look at me that way. What's so bad about trying to be useful?"

My fingers close around her throat. I shake her.

"What's so bad?"

"Nothing."

"What?"

"Nothing."

"I can't hear you."

"Nothing!"

"So why didn't you knock? Instead you aggravated me. Is that any way to treat someone *you trust*?"

She studies her hands distractedly, notices that her lips are dry, and passes a purple tongue over them again and again.

"I didn't want to disturb you."

"You wouldn't have disturbed me."

My fingers loosen their grip on her throat and slide across her cheeks, calmingly. She snuggles her neck into her shoulders; her eyelids contract every time my hands touch her, as if she is expecting me to rip her skin off.

"You must call for me. It is important. Naturally, everyone is shy when they are not in their own home; nobody wants to abuse another's hospitality and consideration. That is indeed a praiseworthy and dignified attitude. But here, with me, it's different. I am the simplest person imaginable, do you understand?"

"All right . . . calm down."

"I *am* calm. What makes you think I'm not calm? Look, my hands are not trembling, my voice is quiet. I am perfectly calm; there is no reason for me not to be calm."

My hand moves back to her throat.

"You should never make statements without weighing them first. It is unwise, unreasonable."

I take her by the throat again, violently. She cries out, frantic now, and tries to break free.

"Shush!" I put a finger to my lips.

Shouting upsets me. The sound makes me feel as though my head were exploding. I hate noise—nothing is more intolerable to me. I warned Cousin K many a time about this. But K could not have cared less. Worse, she would ratchet it up. Just to irritate me. She screamed down the well deliberately, a din fit to wake the dead.

"Shhhhhh!"

She recoils, pressing herself against the wall and clearly wishing she could pass through it.

"Are you going to knock?"

"Yes, yes . . ."

She knocks on the wall.

"Not right now. There's no hurry—we have plenty of time. It's only three in the morning. First I'm going back to my room. You should wait a while before you knock. No more than two knocks. I am an especially attentive person. I refuse to have anything repeated for me; I would feel inadequate. I shall come at once. Punctuality is the politeness of the gods. You'll say—you'll say whatever you like. That you are still hungry, or that you'd like to chat for a while, or that you are thirsty. I'll go and fetch you a glass of water. If you want, I'll fetch you a fountain in the palm of my hand. That should tell you how far you are from disturbing me."

My fingers draw inspiration from her hair, becoming more skilled with every stroke; I am tenderness incarnate.

"You mustn't say thank you."

She nods, choking.

"You'll say nothing. A modest woman is a silent woman."

Tears slide down her cheeks. I feel some on my own. It is a moment of great solemnity. So I do not console her. One does not intrude on a woman in tears; rather, one learns.

I am moved, shaken. It is almost as though I am forgiving her, as though I am capable of accepting, feeling compassion, sharing. Perhaps hope lies in that: in being useful, in being noticed, in *being* . . . My mother would shoo me away whenever I tried to help her. "Don't touch that vase! You'll only knock it over. Just like the other ones." But I am not clumsy—just absentminded. Sometimes I forget what I am holding, and it slips out of my hands. That was probably what happened at the edge of the well. Perhaps K just slipped from my hands.

"Don't move," I tell the girl.

White with fear, she claps clenched fists to her breast, then produces a few strangled sobs followed by long cowlike groans.

"Hey!"

My cry silences her, forcing her to go and huddle in the corner of the room.

"I'm going to leave now . . . I'm leaving. Don't forget, I'm just next door."

18

ALL OF A sudden I hear her door open.

I rush out.

She is racing for the staircase.

"Stop!"

She runs down the stairs, stumbles, and falls.

I stand at the top of the staircase like a mythic being on a cloud, arms outstretched in a histrionic pose. My titanic command roars forth across the entire planet:

"GET BACK HERE!!!"

Had day and night come together in an eclipse and veiled my eyes, had a thunderbolt, prompted by my sublime gesture, chosen to strike me down, or had my mother picked this precise moment to come home, I believe I would have forgiven everything.

She is crawling toward the bolted front door and hammering on it with her fists.

"Come back! Come back up to your room!"

She refuses to hear me, to listen to reason. Fury courses through me. I go to her, grab her by the hair, push her down and trample her. She cries out, pleads, struggles, kisses my hands, my feet, humiliating herself utterly . . .

"Don't kill me! Please, oh please, I've done nothing to you . . ."

The ungrateful bitch! I redouble my onslaught, laughing. My laughter frightens me. I do not recall laughing ever in my life. She crawls to the stairs and hoists herself up painfully. Blood quivers on her burst lips and dribbles from her chin; her hands wander in confusion.

"That's right. Please, go on up . . . Up, please, into your room."

She struggles to her feet, clinging to the banister, her hair a tumbled dark mass.

I no longer recognize her.

A pitiful specter, she is keeling over before my eyes; she disappoints me.

I shut her in her room. And lock the door.

19

S HE KNOCKS.

Two barely audible scratchings at the wall.

I am capable of hearing the frantic scrambling of a jerboa miles and miles away. My sleepless nights have taught me to discern the slightest rustle, the slightest movement of air in the manor. From attic to cellar, not a thing escapes me. Ever on highest alert, I would be furious to be caught off guard. I have never felt at home in the manor: it has always been unknown territory.

I go back to her.

She is crouched in her corner, hands between her thighs, blouse spattered with blood.

"I thought I heard you call for me."

She nods.

"I felt sure someone was knocking on the wall. So I was not mistaken."

She wipes her nose on her wrist and, swallowing hard, shakes her head. Tears streak her face like the marks of a whip. I am stunned to realize that things have come to this. She could have been waited on like a sultaness. She would have been laughing with joy by now. But she proved unable to seize the chance. Perhaps that explains her poverty, why she had to humiliate herself to survive. People do not always grasp the opportunities within their reach. Not because they don't see them, but because they don't believe in them. Luck and fate are matters of attitude; those who agonize over them have only themselves to blame.

"Do you need something?"

She swallows her saliva convulsively before nodding. Without conviction. Without even looking me in the eye. I fear she has lost faith in me. A pity, if so—a terrible waste.

I help her: "It's hot."

"I—I'm thirsty," she manages to answer.

At last!

I run all the way down to the kitchens. I feel saved, exorcised. I return holding a tray up high with *a pitcher of water as full as the moon*. She notices neither the height nor the fullness. Trapped in her fright, her chin to her chest, she is hopelessly uncouth.

I serve her. With genuine pleasure. Unselfishly. Her hand accepting the glass of water floods me with a sense of infinite *plenitude*.

She drinks. Choking.

I watch her quenching her thirst like a painter watching the welcome signs of his genius coming to light on a canvas. I am *happy*.

"You see? That was so simple."

She hands the glass back to me, her eyes glued to the floor.

"Knock as often as you like," I tell her before taking my leave. "It won't bother me."

20

THE WIND HOWLS in the corridors. Like a werewolf, its breath sulfurous beneath the full moon. Now and again I fancy I see it plunging into my room, pirouetting above my bed, then whirling wildly downstairs to the hallway, there to rejoin the poltergeists, jeering and conspiratorial, that I can hear tormenting drapes, ferreting in armoires, and sporting with rickety doors. Outside, the gate clatters madly and the trees, tearing out their hair, assume terrifying shapes . . . I lie stretched out on my bed, hands clasped beneath my chin. I wait . . .

In my mind's eye I see a peaceful beach lapped by fleeting little waves . . .

I almost doze off.

I am alerted by sounds at once grotesque and unremarkable. Returning to her room, I find her trying to force the window. Drawers strew the floor, tragic as shipwrecks . . . I am outraged. She freezes, opens her mouth, but fails to cry out.

"What's all this?" I inquire affably.

"Let me leave. Oh please let me leave and go home."

"You are at home here."

Her frail shoulders shake; she buries her face in her hands, exhausted, desolate, incredulous.

"It's not possible," she moans. "It's all wrong; I have to wake up . . . Yes, that's it," she adds, "it's all a mistake. You are going to wake up soon, girl. This is just a bad dream. Don't let it get to you."

Touched by this monologue, I go to her with open arms, ready now for reconciliation . . .

"Get away from me!" she cries, shuddering with disgust. "Don't you dare touch me. Keep your filthy paws off me. I can't stand any more."

I take her by the shoulders. As you might a friend. As my brother used to do to me long ago. She pushes me away and flees toward the door. This rejection hurts my feelings, yet I do not hold it against her. I *understand*. I make no attempt to catch her, much less chase after her; I simply follow her. My step is serene, measured; I am calm.

"I'm not a monster," I tell her without animosity. "I am just like anyone else. I'm a soul in torment, and I have my pride. What you're doing is not right."

She ends up in the kitchens and, finding no way of escape, overturns a chair in a fit of pique; penned in, she barricades herself behind the table.

"Why are you running away from me? Do I have the plague? Have I done you any wrong? Or made any demands on you at all?"

"This can't be happening. I've got to wake up."

"I wait on you, and you turn away; I talk to you, and you ignore me; I try to be helpful, and you act as though I weren't there. Where's the harm in wanting to help out, lend a hand or show a little generosity? All I want is to believe I'm as human as anyone else."

"You are mad . . . *Mad!*"

That word!

Such a cyclone of a word, so vile, so arbitrary.

"You see what I mean?" I ask her, sick at heart.

COUSIN K LAUGHED uproariously. My cat had just scratched me—an unwise act, treacherous and foul. Cousin K used to gambol in the orchards, restoring to them what the ravages of time had taken away. The hillside awoke at her laughter: the trees were no longer gibbets, the rocks no longer marabouts, the river no longer a miserable trough . . . With K gone, everything reverted to form: the sun scorching, the wind sighing, and the patron saints of the place mortified. My cat should never have sunk his filthy claws into me. He was nothing but a stray quadruped from the alley—even less than that, in fact, for it was I who made and unmade him according to the circumstances. He might just as easily have died of hunger or been run over by a car . . . "I'll never marry a boring person of your sort," K would say to put me in my place. "I'm going to marry a Moroccan prince. I'll have a splendid jewel-inlaid carriage with two disdainful footmen perched on it, and an enormous palace with fountains all around it and as many eunuchs as courtiers on hand. There'll be festivities every night, and every morning a fantasia; you'll be so jealous. If you come to me on bended knee I'll order my guards to chase you away, and if you are caught lurking about my gardens the sultan will have you beheaded . . . Only a woman cursed would marry a boy who never has a word to say for himself." Whenever K shut me out in this way the sky fell; I felt I tainted the earth merely by standing on it . . . How beautiful she was! I never tire of telling myself just how beautiful. Her eyes were springs from which ecstasy drew water.

When she ran — an antelope! — with ribbons like flowers in her hair, her dress would fly up and reveal her panties, blue as a slice of sea tight against her skin . . . If only she could have behaved properly! But that was too much to ask of Cousin K. There was a demon in her head and she lied like the devil. It was she who broke the china vase. "If I hadn't ducked," she sobbed, "he would have scarred me for life with it." My cousin's tears were a true work of art. Ulysses himself would have fallen for them. "I've told you a thousand times not to touch that vase," my mother screeched, taking me by the ear and slapping me. In front of *her* — who reveled in it. In protest I picked up a shard of the vase and swallowed it . . . *Mad! You're mad! . . .*

"YOU SEE WHAT I mean?" I ask. Then, in a toneless, almost conciliatory voice: "Why do you make statements without first weighing their implications? After all, what do you, personally, know about madness?"

She backs away. What does she hope to achieve by that? Is it to pull herself together? To retract what she has just said? There are impulsive acts that cannot be corrected, but one must take responsibility for them. Suddenly the light in her eyes shatters like a mirror; the splinters shear my brain; it feels like an electric shock. Moving of its own accord, my hand grasps the knife. I am aware of the disproportion of the act, of its tragic potential; some-where, in the chaos, I want to let it drop, but I do not insist. The blade gleams, my arm rebels. *It is written.* Her flesh cedes at the first thrust. With revolting ease. Nothing is frailer than life: such vulnerability! A reflex, just one, suffices; the blows that follow are pure spite.

I go on striking for an eternity. My arm in its frenzy is almost dislocated. Neither the blood splashing the wall and running over my clothes, nor the girl's glazed stare, nor the stupefaction on her face, nor even the gate no longer clattering outside and the ensuing silence can bring me back to my senses. I keep repeating to myself, in the depths of my agony, that even had I truly wanted to I would not have changed a thing.

AFTERWORD | *Safe in Hell*

ROBERT POLITO

For all the irrepressible lyricism, you edge into *Cousin K* suspiciously, the way a traveler might take stock of a foreign yet implausibly predictable vista. Part diary, part rhapsody, every detail and inflection we encounter in the novel registers wrong—perhaps because they also register too right, too neat, too luxurious. From our anonymous narrator's assertion at the outset of his rueful freedom:

> The truth is, I can keep everything, just as I can reject it all. The choice is mine. Just as I am free to forget this story, I am free to tell it as I see fit. It is my story. I can give it any moral I like. Or none.

through his recollection of his monotonous days:

> My morning is as agonizing as it is futile: an island lost in a sea of renunciation. Its sun burns me; its prospect makes me nauseous. I get up, and then what? Go where, do what? My two-way mirror is my glass cage. I can pound on it until I pass

out, no one will hear me. In any case, no one notices me. My morning is a desert where no soul stirs. It brings me nothing. I expect nothing from it; in this sense we are even.

to his vision of his vacant future:

I'm not interested in hopping a moving train, in heading toward fresh disappointments. Nor am I awaiting the redemptive return of some Messiah. People unsettle me. Tomorrows do nothing for me. The turpitude of the world doesn't begin to affect me. I have no more respect for a dying dream than for the leaf of a plane tree turned brown by the fall. I stay behind my mirror, unassailable, curled up in my solitude, and listening—indiscreet, perhaps, but harmless. . . I listen to the night casting anchor in my insomniac soul, the wrinkles fissuring my brow, and the white threads of anguish weaving their web around my breath.

Imprisoned in weariness, in broken promises and dead years, I often peer at length into the half-light without knowing why, mounting watch over the silence for signs of I know not what.

—has alienation ever *sounded* so charming, so resplendent? Is that "mirror" hard fact, for instance, or fancy metaphor? Is he only suggestively "imprisoned," or really inside a prison? Also, as we continue reading, what is this mysterious "manor" he keeps invoking, or that curiously abstract village of Douar Yatim? Where are we? Who, in fact, is talking here? The lyricism seems a trap set for us, yet why, and to what purpose?

Then, perhaps *because* of that irrepressible lyricism, we stop questioning every anguished and sumptuous confession, and start to overhear what we suspect we're not supposed to hear, as though our narrator were simultaneously discovering and

82

disguising his story as he set it down. We assemble the puzzle of his childhood almost inadvertently. The brutal murder of his father as a traitor:

> My father died on the eve of the Great Day. I was five years old. I was the one who found him hanging from an S-hook in the stable, naked from head to toe, his eyes gouged out, his sex in his mouth.

His remote mother, a genius of refusals and exquisite disappointments:

> My mother is gone, who knows where. She doesn't need to tell me where she goes. Yesterday was her birthday. I put a flower on the mantelpiece, just where she keeps her keys. This morning, I found the flower in the same place, drooped and dying.

His casually superior brother, Amine:

> Before long Amine was in the courtyard. Splendid in his officer's uniform. So imposing was the figure he cut that sky and earth were alike obscured.
>
> My mother could not contain herself. She had waited for this moment in pain. Her suffering was even greater now that he was here. Her eyes bespoke childbirth; her joined hands recalled the praying Virgin. She could move neither forward nor back. She tottered, she staggered, she reeled. She overdid it.
>
> And then at last she broke free: "My hero!" she cried.

Yet soon these situations too prompt mistrust and incredulity—though not because they look so implausible, but once again on account of their nagging familiarity. Are there psychological alibis more stock and ready-made than the early death of a father, a resistant mother, and crushing sibling rivalry? We seem to have stumbled onto still another booby trap, our narrator slyly rigging the mechanism with soul-stirring clichés.

Finally, *Cousin K* emerges as a confession of destructive obsession, first for the narrator's nine-year-old city cousin:

> My mother is wearing a scout's neckerchief. This means that she has been honored yet again by the local militants. I had a scout's neckerchief once. My brother gave it to me. I never wore it, but it meant a lot just to have it. I hid it in a cubbyhole in my wardrobe, sure that no one would find it there. By some unknown magic, Cousin K eventually ferreted it out. She liked it and wanted to keep it. I hoped she would humor me a bit—allow me to think I was capable of *giving*. But when I pretended to want it back, she flung it in my face and pushed me against the wall, screaming: "I didn't ask you for the moon! Here, you can eat your flea-ridden rag for all I care! And don't you dare say another word to me ever again."
>
> I was completely unnerved. This was not what I wanted; she had misunderstood. Watching her rage against me, I was panic-stricken. And as she wagged her finger, I thought that if God had chosen to make me anything at all except this puppet that a nine-year-old girl was tearing limb from limb, I would not have disappointed him.

And later, for the woman he comes to believe resembles her, an unnamed woman he rescues after she is tossed from a car, and then locks up in his brother's room. Both find terrible ends. Yet even this obsessive, vengeful violence isn't a last-ditch lunge past our narrator's prior subterfuge and pretense to the ultimate ground zero William Burroughs tagged naked lunch—"a frozen moment when everyone sees what is on the end of every fork"—but only his ultimate retreat into noir formula, and one more of his trapdoor cons. When in his humiliation he recasts his cousin K as a "she-devil"—"K was mean and self-centered, rancorous, spiteful. A she-devil"—or furiously brands the abused woman he's abducted an "ungrateful bitch" after she struggles to flee his beating, it's as if he has somehow escaped his fate in Douar Yatim for the familiar postures of a James M. Cain or Jim Thompson novel, and thus can slyly deflect any guilt for his actions, and instead blame his victims.

The soothing and unsettling lyricism, the mournful and risible psychology, and the vivid shards of crime novel commonplaces: there is no solid or comfortable place for a reader to sit. *Cousin K* inevitably carries a Shakespearean tilt—a novel written by a man (Mohammed Moulessehoul) in the guise of a woman (Yasmina Khadra) who created a man who hates women—and along the continuum of Khadra/Moulessehoul's fiction so far hovers midway between the hot dust of *The Swallows of Kabul* and the shadows of his Inspector Llob detective series. But whether a tone poem splintering into noir, or noir exploded into poetry, it's a beautiful ride to the void.